Ellie
&
The Rainy Day

Kimberly Davis-Peters

Illustrated by Jasmine Mills

Dedication

For my beautiful, amazing, smart, funny, and fabulous Lael – you inspire me to reach farther than I ever imagined. This one's for you.

Ellie woke up with excitement.

She had so many fun things to do outside and could not wait to get started.

Ellie expected to see the sun bright and shining when she climbed out of bed. Instead, there were cloudy, gray skies and the pitter-patter sound of raindrops.

Ellie decided that her day was ruined. **"Ohh no!"** She wailed.

"What's wrong, sweetie?" Asked Mommy.

"It's raining, and now I can't do anything fun," Ellie pouted.

"Just because it's raining doesn't mean we can't have fun. Let me show you," said Mommy.

They put on their raincoats and boots to head outside.

Looking around at the raindrops falling around them, Ellie wondered what fun they could have.

Suddenly, Mommy began to jump up and down in a puddle. Water splashed all over them with each jump. Ellie began jumping in a puddle of her own, laughing as the water splashed against her raincoat.

They hopped from puddle to puddle, laughing and splashing all the way.

"This is fun!" Ellie exclaimed.

They giggled the most when Daddy came home and splashed them as he drove the car into the driveway.

Ellie wondered what other fun things they could do.

Next, Ellie and Mommy twirled their umbrellas and sang to the rain.

"Hello, rain! How are you? The sky is gray, and raindrops are blue. Soon, the clouds will go away, and the sun will come out again!"

Heading back inside, Ellie thought their rainy day fun had come to an end.

"Now, I'll make a perfect, rainy day lunch for you," Mommy said.

Before long, soup and sandwiches were ready for them to eat.

"What a yummy rainy day lunch!" Ellie said while she happily took a big bite of her sandwich.

Later in the afternoon, Ellie painted a picture of herself and Mommy splashing together in the rain puddles.

She named it Rainy Day Art.

The sun began to peek through the clouds as the rain slowly came to an end.

When the rain stopped, Mommy took Ellie by the hand and they went outside.

"There is one more fun thing I want to show you," Mommy said, pointing to the sky and telling Ellie to look up high.

Ellie looked up and saw so many beautiful colors! She asked Mommy what it was.

"That is a rainbow," said Mommy. "Oh, wow!" Ellie said with a wide smile.

At nighttime, they put on their pajamas and got ready for bed.

Mommy tucked Ellie snuggly under the covers. With a sleepy yawn, Ellie began to close her eyes

"So, how did you enjoy your rainy day?" Mommy asked.

Ellie gave a tired smile and mumbled, "I guess rainy days can be fun after all."

She began to snore softly and soon, Ellie was fast asleep.

About the Author

Kimberly Davis-Peters has always loved to read the stories found between the pages of a good book. Eager to share the love of reading with her little one, Kimberly was struck by the limited number of stories featuring African American characters and became inspired to create children's books to help meet this need in the reading community.

Kimberly resides with her family in Columbus, Ohio. She is a passionate writer and currently working on new stories for children.

Follow Kimberly on Instagram & Facebook: @Author_KDP

Dear reader:

Thank you for reading *Ellie & the Rainy Day*. The adventures are only beginning, so if you'd like to follow along, sign up for my reader list at www.Elliesbookshop.com, where you'll get special notifications and offers as new books are released.

If you enjoyed reading this book, please visit the site where you purchased it to leave an honest review and tell a friend. Your feedback is important to me and will help other readers!

With Love & Gratitude,

Kimberly Davis-Peters

Made in the USA
Columbia, SC
07 May 2021

37468844R10015